This Little Tiger book belongs to:

_____

_____

_____

For Kath, Justine, and Andrea
~ C. F.

For Dusty
~ R. T.

LITTLE TIGER PRESS
1 The Coda Centre, 189 Munster Road,
London SW6 6AW
www.littletigerpress.com

First published in Great Britain 2004
by Little Tiger Press, London
This edition published 2012

ISBN 978-1-84895-576-9

Printed in China

10 9 8 7 6 5 4 3 2 1

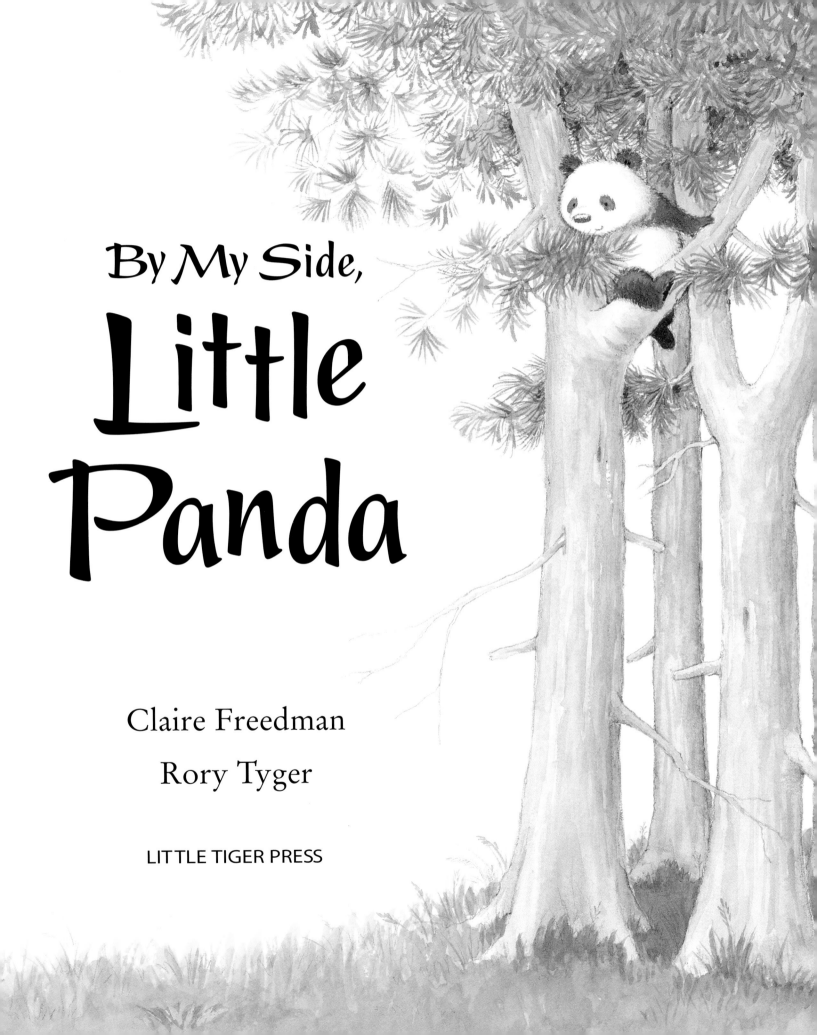

By My Side, Little Panda

Claire Freedman

Rory Tyger

LITTLE TIGER PRESS

Little Panda and his mother did everything together.
Together they explored the mountain tops,
where the snow lay too deep to melt.

Together, they splashed in icy streams,
startling tiny, shiny fish . . .

and rolled down grassy slopes,
carpeted with early spring flowers.

And as the first stars peeped out above
the snowy crags, they were still together,
snuggled up, cozy and warm.

"The world is full of wonders for
a brave little panda bear like you,"
said Mother Panda. "You'll discover
echoing caves where butterflies hide.
You'll play in sparkling waterfalls, and
climb trees so high you can almost
touch the clouds!"

"Will I really do all that?" cried
Little Panda.

"One day!" Mother Panda laughed.

And soon Little Panda was asleep,
dreaming of dancing butterflies!

Springtime passed by, and the days grew warmer. Little Panda was getting bigger every day.

One morning, when the sun shone and summer was in the air, Little Panda asked, "What are we doing today?"

"Why don't you play in the meadow?" his mother replied. "You could go splashing in the stream."

"On my own?" said Little Panda a bit doubtfully. "Without you?"

"We could go to the Great Pine Forest if you'd prefer," Mother Panda said.

"Together?" Little Panda asked.

"Together!" his mother agreed.

Little Panda had never been in the
Great Pine Forest before.

Golden monkeys with bright blue
faces leaped through the leafy trees.
Soft gray musk deer peeped out from
the misty shadows and colorful birds
fluttered across their path.

"Look, Mommy, look!" Little Panda
cried, his eyes shining with excitement.

Deeper in the forest Little Panda's
mother paused. "This is the sweetest,
juiciest bamboo on the whole mountain!"
she said. "Shall we climb this tree and
pick some?"

"But it's so tall!" gasped Little Panda.

"Don't worry. I'll be right beside
you," his mother smiled.

The two pandas climbed to the top of the swaying tree. "I'm good at climbing, aren't I?" Little Panda said. "Very good!" his mother nodded.

They sat in the branches and munched and crunched on the best bamboo Little Panda had ever tasted!

"I've seen so many new things today," Little Panda said. "The forest is very big and exciting!"

"I know," Mother Panda laughed. "You're going to have a lot of fun exploring it all!"

The next day, the two bears walked down
to the Great Pine Forest once more.

Little Panda heard a rustling sound in the
trees. A young panda peek-a-booed him
through the leaves. Little Panda laughed!

"Would you like to go and play with him?"
asked Mother Panda.

Little Panda hesitated . . .

"I'll be here if you need me!" she said.

The friendly panda peeped his head out through the leaves again! Little Panda clambered up through the branches to join him.

Little Panda and his new friend chased
each other through the tall trees and played
hide-and-seek in the thick bamboo.

They raced down to the stream
and splashed in the cool water.

They rolled dry and lolled in the grass together. It was all great fun!

Then, suddenly, Little Panda heard his mother calling him.

"Time to go home!"

"What, already?" Little Panda cried, scrambling back through the trees.

"We'll come again tomorrow!" Mother Panda laughed.

Mother Panda and Little Panda headed
back up the mountain.

"Did you have fun with your new
friend today?" she asked him.

"Oh, yes!" cried Little Panda happily,
bouncing over the rocks. "We chased each
other all through the forest! We climbed
the biggest tree you've ever seen!"

Little Panda gazed out across the valley, glowing pink under the setting sun.

"Tomorrow I'm going to explore all the way over to the Big River!" he told his mother sleepily.

Mother Panda smiled as she wrapped her arms around Little Panda. He closed his eyes and snuggled deep into her warm fur.

Soon stars began to twinkle in the darkening sky. But Little Panda didn't see them. He was fast asleep!